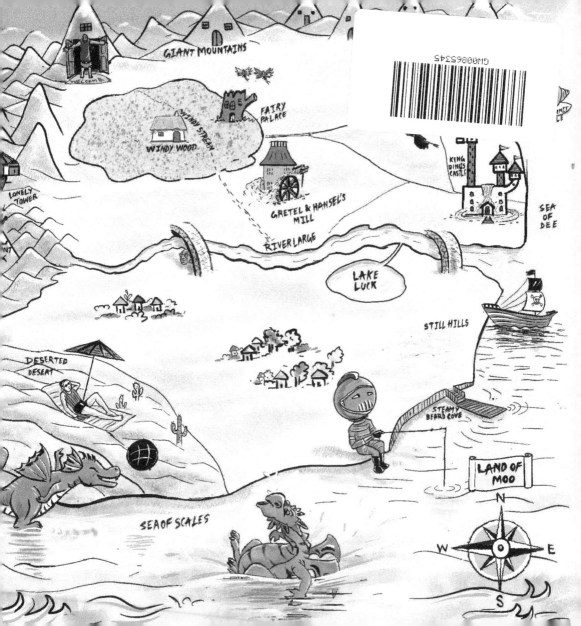

Dedication

To my girls: Katie, Ezealia and Meribelle.
My inspirations. Love Dad/Al-x

A CIP catalogue record for this title is
available from the British Library.

ISBN: 978-1-83934-197-7

Bumblebee Books is an imprint of
Olympia Publishers.

First Published in 2021

Bumblebee Books
Tallis House
2 Tallis Street
London
EC4Y 0AB

Printed in Great Britain

www.olympiapublishers.com

Mr Wiz and the Dragon

Written by Alex Stears

Bumblebee Books
London

In the land of Moo, in the middle of Windy Wood, lives Mr Wiz the wizard.

He's not a very good wizard, but he's definitely a wizard!
He's not very good because when he tries to cast spells they somehow always go a bit wrong.

For example, Mr Wiz doesn't like his name much (Wez Wiz), so once he tried to change it using one of his spells.

Unfortunately, all he managed to do was turn his favourite chair into a very uncomfortable rock!

One day, while Mr Wiz was pottering around in his kitchen, there was a knock on his front door.

When he answered the door, there, standing in front of him, was a bright yellow dragon.

"Hello," said the dragon, "are you Mr Wiz the wizard?"

"Yes, yes I am. And who are you?" replied Mr Wiz.

"I'm Mustard the dragon," said Mustard the dragon. "I was wondering if you could help? Everyone says that I'm a very ordinary dragon. So I want to become the biggest dragon in the world ever!"

"Come in, come in," said Mr Wiz happily. "Well, I can try and help you, but I must warn you that my spells don't always go to plan."

"That's OK, please just try your very best." said Mustard.

So Mr Wiz pulled out his bent wand and said the magic words, "Bagoo bagoo bag."
Mustard closed his eyes.

There was a puff of smoke.
"Did it work?" he asked hopefully.
"Well… not quite," Mr Wiz said, looking Mustard
up and down.
Mustard looked in the mirror.

"I'm a unicorn! A unicorn!" exclaimed Mustard disappointedly.

"Don't you like being a unicorn?" asked Mr Wiz.

"Well, I do love the purple horn but I don't want to be a unicorn! I want to be a BIG HUGE DRAGON! The biggest one in the world EVER!" replied Mustard.

"Sorry. OK, well I'll try again," said Mr Wiz, and he said the magic words and waved his bent wand, "Bagoo bagoo bag."
Mustard shut his eyes again.
There was another puff of smoke.

"Did it work this time?" Mustard again asked hopefully.

"What did you say you wanted to be again?" asked Mr Wiz.

"A big huge dragon! The biggest in the world ever!" said Mustard.

"Well… not quite then," replied Mr Wiz staring at Mustard.

Mustard opened his eyes and looked in the mirror.

"I'm a monkey! A monkey!" exclaimed Mustard. "Don't you like being a monkey?" asked Mr Wiz. "Well, I do like bananas and swinging around, but I don't want to be a monkey! I want to be a BIG HUGE GIGANTIC DRAGON! The biggest one in the world EVER!" replied Mustard.

"Oh," said Mr Wiz, "sorry about that. I'll try again." And with that he waved his bent wand and said the magic words again, "Bagoo bagoo bag." There was yet another puff of smoke and Mustard shut his eyes.

"How about now?" asked Mustard with his eyes still shut.

"What did you say you wanted to be again?" asked Mr Wiz once more.

"I said I wanted to be a big huge enormous gigantic dragon. Not a unicorn, or a monkey, but a BIG HUGE ENORMOUS GIGANTIC DRAGON! The biggest one in the world EVER!"

"In that case… not quite."

"Why? What am I now?"

"Well, you're a… a… giant!" shouted Mr Wiz.

Mustard opened his eyes.

He had clouds all around his head and a small bird perched on his nose. Mustard looked down.

"Arrrgggghhh!" he shouted. "I don't like heights. Quick, turn me back to normal!"

"Are you sure? You are very big now!" asked Mr Wiz.

"Yes I'm sure. Turn me back, turn me back!" cried Mustard.

"OK, I'll try." and again Mr Wiz waved his bent wand and said the magic words, "Bagoo bagoo bag."

There was yet another puff of smoke and Mustard closed his eyes.

"Did it work?" he asked once more.

"Almost," said Mr Wiz

Mustard looked in the mirror.

"Well, I am me but I've got a purple horn!"

"Sorry, would you like me to try again?"

"No, I love it!" exclaimed Mustard. "Thank you, Mr Wiz. I'm not a big huge enormous gigantic dragon, but I love being me, especially with my new purple horn!"

Mustard was happier than ever.

And just like magic Mr Wiz and Mustard became the best of friends!

About the Author

Alex was born and raised in Northampton, UK. After going travelling, he and his wife, Katie, moved to Hong Kong for work. Still in Hong Kong, Alex is now a very proud father of two wonderful girls, and has the great joy of being a stay-at-home dad.

9 781839 341977